The Second

A Practical Guide to Establishing Church Structure

Kirby Clements

DEDICATION

To my wife, Sandra,
for her love, patience and encouragement.

TABLE OF CONTENTS

FOREWORD

How do strong leaders work together in one vision? Who makes the final decision when twenty-two strong-willed men and women in leadership have various opinions over the direction of a ministry? What are the keys to survival for an associate pastor facing what seems to be overwhelming conflicts between those over him and those whom he leads? Dr. Kirby Clements answers these and other questions in his book, **The Second,** a practical guide to establishing church structure.

I commend this book by Dr. Clements. He has worked beside me as an assistant in the office of a Bishop serving hundreds of churches. The guidelines he espouses are those he has learned well through daily experiences as a trouble-shooter in discerning root problems in local ministries. His own experiences serving on a multifaceted staff led by a powerfully diverse presbytery have also contributed significantly to the insights of this book.

One of the greatest dangers facing Church leaders today is to surround themselves with "yes" men and women. At the same time, unity of purpose and direction is the secret of successful ministry. How can a ministry have both diversity and unity? The process of discovering that answer makes all the difference in the impact and scope of influence that any local church will know.

Indeed, God is calling for maturity, integrity and accountability from His leaders in this hour. We need to learn quickly the lessons the Holy Spirit is teaching us, and move with confidence as bold witnesses to the righteousness, peace and joy that only comes in serving our Lord and King.

Our King Cometh!
Bishop Earl Paulk

INTRODUCTION

"There are four things which are little upon the earth, but they are exceedingly wise; the ants are a people not strong, yet they prepare their meat in the summer; the conies are but a feeble folk, yet they make houses in the rocks; the locusts have no king, yet they go forth all of them in bands; the spider taketh hold with her hands, and is in kings' palaces."

Proverbs 30:24-28

Every system of accomplishment exhibits some order, design and purpose. *The Second* is a compilation of experiences, observations and insights into the cooperative relationship that must exist between primary leadership and the associates and staff. Leaders, as visionaries, must lead without unnecessary distractions. Associates and staff personnel, as implementors, must comprehend their cooperative roles in the productive process.

A ministry is no greater than its ability to hear from God and to obey. Without a vision, a ministry's direction can either go nowhere or everywhere. It can become stagnated without the energy of direction or it can become encumbered with needless activity without a gravitational purpose. And of course, visions are of no consequence unless they can be properly articulated and given practical expressions which are capable of enlisting the participation of people.

Leadership
A Profile

For any organization to survive and to be successful there must be identifiable leadership. These leaders must lead and point the way for all to follow. They must be willing to make decisions, to assume the responsibility for others and to elicit the trust and confidence of those who follow. A leader must be able to motivate others to a level of performance and productivity. People are capable of great exploits whenever true leaders enlist their cooperation.

There are no distinct personality types, voice inflections or physical statures that make one leader more effective than another. Some sound like giants and some squeak. Some have the stature and charm of kings, while others have the elegance of a bull in a china shop.

Some leaders are seemingly more emotionally and physically constituted to accept stress and pressure than others, but all adapt to these challenges in their own ways. Some are gifted with insight and a knack for understanding people and their problems. Others compensate for what appears to be a lack of certain intrinsic qualities by establishing an organized structure that allows them to administrate their leadership through delegating responsibility. When the structure is well organized and job performance functions well enough to ensure accountability, then the leader administrates the oil into the machine.

Observable qualities in leadership that are called great are: first, empathy and acceptance of those they lead. Leaders can project themselves into another's shoes and identify with their problems. Second, a tolerance of imperfections. Leaders can accept the abilities and performance of the individual, though at times they may reject the products of their efforts because they recognize the potential of some and the limitations of others. Third, leaders possess an awareness and sensitivity to the signals emitted by people and the environment. They must discern the times, seasons, moods and attitudes of people and the circumstances they encounter. Since leaders are subject to extreme pressures and at times are forced to function under adverse situations, their survival depends upon their ability to adapt. Building programs, the problems of increasing demands and the frailty of human nature can be an unhealthy mix. How do leaders survive?

My mentor in the ministry, Bishop Earl Paulk, related to me a truth that has sustained him for well over forty years in the ministry and as the senior pastor of a 12,000 member church with tremendous local, national and international responsibilities. He said, "In order to survive each day, you must learn to put some things on the shelf of your mind until another day. Some things you leave on the shelf forever." He advocates a systematic neglect of the less important for the urgent, and a turning of the other cheek, or even the appointment book or the telephone.

The willingness to withdraw oneself from pressing pursuits and challenges in order to reorient priorities spells survival. Probably more poor decisions are made during times of exhaustion and mental fatigue than are necessary. Balance is a big word in ministry. When a leader is unable to maintain equilibrium, it is advisable to place responsible people around that leader. Other leaders can read the imbalance signals and render legitimate recommendations.

When a leader is functioning in his true calling, there is no burnout. Burnout comes from assuming responsibilities beyond one's calling. However, genuine tension can be equilibrated by learning to change dimensions through something as simple as a movie, exercise or a brief sabbatical.

Since leaders assume a variety of personalities and management styles, it is important to understand these traits. Understanding one's style contributes toward a more productive working relationship and gives insight into the decision-making process. Many ministries establish a plurality of leadership or multiple elders who assist a primal leader. Consequently, decisions are made through the interaction of these different personalities and their leadership styles. Some are bold and aggressive. Others tend to entreat. Some are perennially optimistic, while others get bogged down with the nuts and bolts of pragmatism. Some can sway an entire meeting with charisma, while others chip away with a calculated persistency. The miracle is that all is needed.

The following is a sample of some personality and leadership characteristics:

Type 1: The hearty and optimistic type who is yet tender with an ability to share in the emotions of others. Generally outgoing, friendly and spontaneous. Tremendous motivator, great starter, but not so great as a finisher. Demands allegiance and full cooperation from associates. Will generally make instant decisions and handle challenges courageously.

Type 2: The aggressive, tenacious, self-confident type with a singleness of purpose. Tends to be a keen organizer. Quickly appraises situations. Forceful and dominant. This type rules with an iron hand. Can be blunt, sarcastic, unsympathetic and slow to show approval. Capable of challenging dissonance, but can learn to entreat.

Type 3: The sensitive, emotional type who is creative, analytical and detailed. Tends to be a perfectionist. Can be very demanding of others. Often found to be indecisive for fear of making mistakes. Disdains confrontation and tends to entreat others.

Type 4: The easygoing, good-natured type who tends to be very practical and tenacious. Rarely makes sudden decisions. Tends to be a good organizer.

Obviously, this listing is in no way exhaustive of the many different personality types. However, it is significant to understand the place that personality dynamics play in the decision-making process and the day-by-day interactions of leaders. There is a place for the optimist and the pragmatist, for the aggressor and the entreator.

Among the characteristics that are present in leaders who are called great are awareness and sensitivity—the ability to be responsive to the signals emitted by people, the environment and the Holy Spirit. This sensitivity is the process of becoming protoplasmic or even allergic to one's environment.

Music leaders who have the greatest success seemingly are those gifted with a sensitivity to the spiritual temperature of a meeting. They are able to project or feel with people in such a manner that their choices of musical selections become fluid. They also know when to begin and to end the singing of some of the congregational choruses. It requires discipline to have an ear to the people and the environment, while still maintaining a delicate listening ear to the Holy Spirit. God also has moods. Clariece Paulk, head of the Music and Arts Department of Chapel Hill Harvester Church, a ministry well known for its abundant musical abilities, prepares a worship format of musical selections before each service. Each selection is always subject to change during that service. Since music creates a receptive atmosphere for the subsequent ministry of the Word, the sensitivity of the musical leader to the primal minister in selecting the choruses is essential.

Sensitivity to the Holy Spirit is critical to the ongoing success of any ministry. He modulates the stops, goings and turns of a ministry. It is imperative to respond immediately to Him.

People who are extremely sensitive to the Holy Spirit can also be vulnerable to the activity of other spiritual forces. For example, they may find themselves under great duress in a meeting charged with strife, tension and debate. Furthermore, they *pick up* on the lack of cooperation, resentment or jealousy in a meeting. If they do not correctly process this negative input, they can receive it as a personal affront to them. This reaction leads to hurt, rejection or even anger within themselves.

I recall a minister's wife who perceived that the elders at their church did not care for her. She especially noticed this during the periods of their building program. When she would enter a meeting of the elders with her husband, she would become sensitive to the feelings and reactions of the elders toward some of their decisions or discussions. She would interpret these *signals* as arrows sent her way. She labored under great duress for many months until she recognized the problem. While everyone else in those meetings projected a sense of cooperation and unity, she was perceiving their lack of unity. She had incorrectly designated herself as the focus of their complaints. She was greatly relieved to know that her sensitivity to the Holy Spirit enabled her to be allergic to other spiritual activity. She began to expose her perceptions to her husband and to another peer minister for their input.

One of the qualities of great leadership is the willingness to make decisions and assume responsibility for others. Those who contemplate the weightiness of their decisions on the destiny of the entire work are at times struck with awe. To think that all the years of labor can be erased by one wrong decision at a strategic moment keeps one in a perennial state of dependency upon the Lord.

As the work grows, new faces are added. A decentralizing of the influence and control of the work occurs. Then there is always the possibility of fragmentation of the ministry. It appears that the ministry is always in a state of jeopardy. That delicate balance between success and failure always exists.

Can you delegate responsibility to others with a comfortable level of confidence that they will properly function? What if the people don't respond during the building program, and the elders turn against it also? When key people who have been a vital part of the work leave, how do we replace them? The apprehension produced by all of these and other factors engenders a degree of insecurity in every leader that cannot be termed a lack of faith. Knowing you are small in your own eyes reminds you that you cannot possibly accomplish the task that has been thrust upon you. The breaking of every new day is filled with many uncertainties. Insecurity is a companion to key leadership.

Insecurities manifest themselves in many different ways. Sometimes it may be the driving force behind a judgmental spirit that consistently finds fault and rarely compliments others. Constant accusation of the actions of others is always divisive or undermining. Criticizing can at times find roots in our own insecurities. There appears to be a very thin line of demarcation between critical and judgmental behavior.

Once again, a multitude of counsel from seasoned eldership is essential in matters of character assessment. Critical and judgmental spirits engender strife among a group because they generate an environment of failure. Displaced motives among associates or staff can greatly hamper the integrity and ongoing productivity of the work if left undetected.

Discernment is the mark of maturity in a ministry.

The human spirit needs encouragement and acknowledgment of good deeds. Since instruction encompasses both correction and encouragement, a delicate balance must be maintained. A healthy ministry, like the one under which I have been privileged to tenure, demonstrates the balance between productive discernment and proper action in dealing with areas of staff relations and functions.

Maintaining the Integrity of Leadership

Ministry consists of a family of people with a mixture of different personalities, perspectives, views, opinions, preferences, motives and methods. The success of the ministry derives—all other things being equal—when the conflicts are minimized and the cooperative efforts are accentuated. Personal ambitions of each individual must be rallied around a common goal or vision. When they are allowed to comprehend how their individual potential, gifts and callings fit into the total scheme of things, a productive process will begin.

Making The Vision Plain

The beginning and continuity of every ministry must be a clearly articulated vision that is comprehensive. It must be given audible, visible and practical expression. It must continually be set before the ministry team until they are able both to articulate and to give some practical expression to it also. The vision becomes the direction and purpose to which every individual labor becomes subordinate.

Ironically, there can only be one major theme at a time. There may be smaller visions that flow out of or in collaboration with the central theme, but they must never be in conflict with it. Too many big fires in a large house will burn down the house. The success of minor themes depends upon their proper alignment with the central theme in such a way as to be complementary. In fact, part of the success of a growing ministry lies in the continuous evolution of sub-themes from the major theme.

Visions or themes are of no consequence unless they can be properly conveyed to those who are called to be *implementors*. The responsibility of the *visionary* is to communicate. Interaction with staff and workers becomes a necessary procedure. Bishop Earl Paulk, senior pastor of Chapel Hill Harvester Church in Decatur, Georgia, a thriving church with local, national and international outreach responsibility, has a clearly articulated vision that has been given visible, audible and practical expressions. (See Bishop Paulk's biography, *The Provoker* by Tricia Weeks; Kingdom Publishers, 1986.)

Ongoing facets of his vision are often articulated during Bishop Paulk's preaching to the entire congregation. The associate staff will extend the vision in their areas of expertise such as publications, covenant communities or home group meetings, and in adjunct teaching sessions available to the congregation. The necessity of providing *grassroots* visionary information to new members and staff who did not have the privilege of participating in the historical experiences of the ministry is absolutely necessary. The key is communication. ". . . Write the vision and make it plain on tablets, that he may run who reads it" (Habakkuk 2:2).

Releasing Ministry
As a ministry grows, associates and other staff members have different backgrounds, perspectives and callings. A willingness on the part of the found-

ing leaders to share responsibilities with others must exist. Decentralization of leadership is absolutely necessary to accommodate the demands of a growing ministry. A successful ministry must address the needs of the young, the elderly, singles, single parents and young families. Social and emotional difficulties, such as the chemically addicted, the homosexual and those who have experienced crisis relationships through death, divorce, etc., must also be addressed.

Each new ministry with its leadership becomes a new channel of influence and authority within the overall ministry. In addition to restoration ministries are also the choir, orchestra, dance and drama groups, as well as school personnel.

A large ministry becomes a delicately constructed sphere, held together ever so carefully by trust, integrity, discernment and communication. Regularly scheduled meetings with pastoral leadership and staff are vital. During these meetings, opportunities are given for the key leaders to give current input regarding ministry priorities and agendas. It is also a time to impart principles regarding staff relations. Top leadership must correct any malfunctions and allow for interaction between the various ministry areas.

At Chapel Hill Harvester Church, primal leadership maintains ongoing involvement in the decision-making processes of every ministry through regular, strategic meetings. In addition, assigned leaders provide a liaison to every ministry. The entire staff meets every Monday morning for briefings, announcements, interdepartmental sharing and prayer. This allows an opportunity for the primal leader to address the entire group.

At other times the associate pastors and key staff leaders meet to discuss the business of the church and ministerial matters. At noon on Wednesday, a staff luncheon is provided where all staff and other leadership fellowship. Once again, this gives an opportunity for the key leadership to address the entire staff. On Friday morning, there is a ministry meeting with the leaders of departments and ministries. It is an effective time for interaction and administering directives for the church.

One of the secrets of successful ministry is effective communication to people so that they can be involved in the process of implementation. To give practical expression to information is to open doors for people to become involved.

When new members join a ministry, there must be an immediate process of soliciting information from them regarding their abilities, experiences and preferences regarding work within the church. Once this information is gathered and processed, it is imperative that the new members become involved at some level. Often, the first involvement may be in home groups or new members' classes. They should also be encouraged to get involved in some aspect of the ministry in the church.

Since the human association factor is significant in attracting people to a church, it is important to develop some levels of friendship with new people. Family relationships and friendships provide strong magnetic attractions bringing new people to the church.

Realism is a key in ministry. Jesus addressed reality and He was not very *religious*. His alleged association with *publicans* and *harlots,* and the manner in which he answered his accusers—"The sick have need of a physician"—give great insight into the *realness* of Jesus. Leaders who are both real and spiritually wise attract people. People can identify with the *humaneness* of a leader, but they also want to hear from God.

However, the leader must not encumber the people with an overabundance of vulnerability concerning his personal struggles and difficulties. Leaders have feet of clay, but they also have the responsibility for leadership. During the early phases of a developing ministry, there is always a tendency for the leader to project himself as *one of the boys* with the congregation. But as the ministry grows and demands increase, there is less opportunity for this interaction.

The recognition of the gifts and callings of staff and associates and the release of these implementors to function at the highest levels of their experience and faith is most challenging. It is clear that a ministry is vulnerable to the insights, decisions and motives of the people it employs. Will they be as dedicated and conscientious toward the people as they are toward the founders? Will they love the people and minister to them in the same manner as the fathers of the work? Since there is no absolute certainty, workers must be proven under conditions of ministry.

My years as a systems equipment engineer with Western Electric taught me the efficacy of uncovering faults in an employee while at the same time aiding in the development of his fullest potential. Since thousands of dollars and hours would be spent in the development of an employee, it was essential to have some insight into his performance potential and his loyalty. Such knowledge is called good business.

Likewise in the staffing procedures of a ministry,

efforts are made to discover people who are ethical, trustworthy and responsible. Inevitably, a battery of tests lie ahead of new recruits. These endurance runs and obstacle courses are actually friends and not foes. They are designed to detect consistency, dedication, zeal and trustworthiness. At times an elder must come beside the new recruit to allow him to open his heart. The conversation may seem subversive, but it provides great wisdom by helping the recruit survive.

The most critical time for a young staff member or associate is whenever principles and practices can be adjusted to enhance his potential. Since peers seemingly communicate more freely with one another than they do with upper levels of leadership, a peer-equal can be a valuable confidant during the developing stages.

The assignment of advisors or liaisons can be most effective in facilitating the needed communication among leadership and staff. This does not suggest the need for a mediator, but it does provide an effective channel of communication during critical periods of staff development.

Associate Leadership

Associates who are added to a ministry may possess talents and abilities unlike those of the primal leadership. This is complementary since it augments the strengths and compensates for the weaknesses. It is practical to employ people who meet the ministry's weaknesses, or non-giftings, rather than its strengths. Of course, this can be threatening to the integrity of the ministry unless associates recognize that their position is to augment the effectiveness of the primal leadership.

Since part of the success of the ministry rests

upon the ability of the key leader to lead without distractions, especially from associates, it is important for the associates to direct the focus of the people toward the key leader in the exercise of his ministry. Associates should never allow themselves to be placed in a competitive posture. Competition at leadership levels forces people to make choices in their allegiance.

Associates should discourage any comparison of leaders among the people ("Saul has killed his thousands, but David has killed his ten-thousands"). The strength of the primal leader should always be enhanced.

As a ministry continues to expand, there is a growing need to decentralize the leadership and delegate responsibilities. However, there is a danger of over-delegation as well as under-delegation. A reluctant leader can easily relinquish the undesirable chores to such an extent that his image as a leader diminishes.

A growing ministry that has an increasing counseling load and a limited pastoral capacity may need to develop more pastors or additional counseling opportunities. It is advisable to view additional counseling opportunities as an extension of the pastorate to maintain the integrity of the ministry.

People tend to develop allegiances to counselors simply because they confide in them during some of the most traumatic periods of their lives. If the counseling department is separated from the pastorate, unnecessary fragmentation often develops. It is important that the pastor be viewed as the leader and the relationship between adjunct leaders be clearly defined as supportive roles.

Since counseling philosophy is a very delicate

issue and a potential source of difficulty, it is advisable that ongoing inter-communication exist between adjunct counselors. A consistency in methodology and principle among counselors in a ministry is mandatory.

One well-known ministry advises its pastors to use principles of counseling rather than give directives. This method allows counselees to assume the direct responsibility for their actions. The counselors are specifically made aware of potential liabilities and legal constraints. This seems to be a rather healthy, safe approach to a growing function required of expanding church ministries.

The threat of losing integrity and continuity looms over any ministry, especially in a period of growth when adding additional staff. Associates lack the experience of the founding leaders and possess gifts and callings that may appear to be different. A clear conceptualization of corporate function must be established. When a primal leader adds an associate who compensates for a non-gifted area in that ministry and his function is influential with the congregation, it is vital that the new ministry be viewed in a complementary posture.

For example, a music or worship leader is added to a growing church. In such a case close interaction between the primal leader and the music leader is mandatory. The new associate must recognize quickly that his primary function is to complement the key leader. There can be no place for independence or flaunting his talents. Since music opens the hearts of the people, the choice of congregational choruses or special songs should be made in collaboration with the speaker.

In some Pentecostal or Charismatic worship

there is a tendency to keep people standing on their feet for extended periods. Those leaders are not sensitive to the complementary place that music should play in preparing people. Instead, the people are exhausted before the ministry of the Word. Sensitivity and communication are still the key.

Associates build confidence in key leadership. They accentuate the strength of the head ministry and keep the focus and allegiance of the congregation from being divided. Competition has no place in the life of a ministry. A leadership that functions together may be under a tremendously powerful *corporate anointing* but the individual leaders functioning autonomously will only become a distraction.

The complementary nature of ministry must be understood and practiced. Often a music leader may have tremendous success in a corporate setting, but lack a similar measure of success alone. The reason for such a difference in performance is the factor of the corporate anointing. Success as part of a corporate body does not always guarantee the same anointing when functioning alone.

On the other hand, when a divine directive comes to set forth a minister who has been functioning under this corporate anointing, there seems to be an *impartation* that produces great success. In essence, there seems to be a proper way to go out and to come in without exerting an independent spirit. And of course, if there is reluctance on the part of the primal leader to release an associate leader once a clearly divine direction is known, much prayer and patience must be exercised. The Lord will surely execute His will in the matter.

Culture

As ministries expand to meet the growing

demands of a rapidly changing society, new challenges arise. Some of these challenges occur as the *complexion* of a ministry changes. Growing churches become a heterogeneous mixture of cultural and ethnic groupings. For the sake of definition, *culture* shall be defined as the customary beliefs, religious, social and material preferences and traits of a group. A mixed-cultural church will reflect a delicate blend of the different cultural expressions of its people.

A mixed-cultural church will have significant homogeneous subcultures within the framework of a culturally heterogeneous church. Which culture will be dominant? Since music is a significant part of any culture, which musical preferences will rule? How do you appease the varied cultural requirements of each group to have expression? The complexities to the problems posed in these questions are unending.

So how can a ministry survive and thrive as its complexion changes? Chapel Hill Harvester Church in Decatur, Georgia, has made tremendous strides in crossing this cultural bridge. With an interracial congregation of 12,000, this church has managed to transcend cultural difference. It is not simply another example of sub-dominant cultures taking on the characteristics of the dominant culture, nor is it a total violation of the integrity of the distinct ethnic and cultural groupings. There is a genuine effort on the part of Blacks, Whites, Hispanics, Orientals and other groups to develop a trans-cultural church.

The praise and worship of Chapel Hill Harvester Church is an interesting blend of cultural expressions. There is neither a predominance of a Black sound nor a country or western sound, but a consortium of hymns, contemporary selections and spiritual songs that combine to represent the congregational musical expressions. The effort is God-centered rather than ethnic-centered in the choices of musical expressions.

Exposing people to new and innovative choices in music increases versatility among a congregation. At times a congregation can exert tremendous control in a service by its response or lack of response. An enthusiastic response carries great weight in influencing a musical leader, as does a less enthusiastic response.

A musical leader must find a delicate balance between God-centered worship and the praise and musical preferences of the congregation. Time, patience, love and perseverance during times of transition will overcome resistance. As new choruses are introduced and opportunity is given for a variety of musical expressions, the trust level of the congregation increases.

Spiritual Authority

Truth generally impacts people in a radical fashion. Its original expression borders on extremes as people desperately attempt to comprehend meaning. Such is the case with the concept of *spiritual authority*. The pendulum on this teaching has swung to extremes. This was not due to the lack of a clear, precise and accurate expression of the revelation by the fathers, but a gradual misconception by the children. It's not in the vine, but in the branches where problems occur. Unfortunately, moves of God are judged by their branches rather than their roots.

Spiritual authority is never dictatorial nor controlling. It is not a concept that engenders bondage nor deprives one of individual liberties. In fact spiritual authority is not even a person. Spiritual authority is an influence in the heavenly or the spiritual realm. ("Jesus I know, Paul I know, but who are you?") *Authority* connotes influence with God and powers and principalities. This authority is conveyed through prayer, preaching, teaching and the implementation of other commissions of God such as worship and praise (David exhibited authority in heavenly places when he played on the stringed instrument).

This authority is not simply resident in the pulpit, but also resides in the congregation. It has no respect to age or tenure. Spiritual authority flows when some people sing or dance. This authority elicits praise and worship in a corporate body of worshipers. This power calls God's people to obedience. It restores the fallen, heals the brokenhearted and opens the prison doors of the captive. Authority is exhibited in the writings of some authors and scribes.

Spiritual authority is displayed whenever God works with an individual or a group. There can even be corporate spiritual authority that resides in a local work or ministry as a whole. Some ministries have no individual expression of this influence, but certainly they exhibit a corporate one.

Pulpit and Congregational Authority

Leaders are called to lead, to establish priorities, to ascertain capabilities among those who are brought alongside them in the implementation of the work. One cannot lead by following. One cannot lead by identifying themselves as one of the people they are called to lead. A necessary space of influence always must separate the leader from the people. This does not eliminate the fellowship nor the light moments that a leader enjoys with the people.

However, there is a degree of vulnerability that a leader only expresses with his peers. This does not prevent a leader from being *real* or *clay* before the people. The exposure of frailties, faults or becoming "one of the boys" does nothing to authenticate leadership. When people need prayer or a touch from a servant of God, they do not seek "one of the guys" to boost their faith. This separation is not assuming an attitude of aloofness or of being unavailable or untouchable. But the leader must adjust his level of vulnerability and commonality.

Leadership is established in many different ways. Those who have public exposure are often viewed in an authoritative posture. Those who speak out publicly are generally viewed by the congregation as having influence. Consequently, prophetic utterances which originate from the congregation may carry as much influence as pulpit leadership. It is important that all prophetic utterances be judged as to their authenticity. The exercising of spiritual gifts publicly must have a proper structure to ensure the proper distinction between false spirits and the Spirit of God. Also, a distinction must be made between zealous activity generated by ignorance of spiritual matters and genuine demonic activity.

The gifts of the Holy Spirit are resident in every Spirit-filled believer. Ministry through spiritual gifts can be administered as the Spirit wills, according to one's measure of faith. People tend to over-emphasize the vocal gifts within the boundary of the Church. Directive leadership must clearly be established in the pulpit. Consequently, directive prophecy will generally be a function of the pastoral leadership and not of the congregation.

The priesthood of believers is an interesting concept. It establishes the principle that all believers have access to the Father by one Spirit. Furthermore, the gifts of the Holy Spirit are resident in every Spirit-filled believer who is commissioned to minister according to the proportion of his faith. "According to your faith, be it unto you" is the promise to every Christian. Yet, there are clear distinctions of faith among ministers that must be recognized.

First of all, directive leadership is clearly established in the pulpit or whatever serves as the focal point of proclamation to the entire group. The accountability for direction in the church rests with the leadership, not with the congregation. Therefore directive prophecy will generally be a function of leadership. Revelation of a vision for direction has a companion faith or authority. The question is not whether there is pulpit or congregational authority, but rather where the accountability before God is.

Revelation and prophecies from the people are valid ("I wish you all spoke in tongues, but even more that you prophesied . . ." 1 Corinthians 14:5). However, accountable direction must reside among the leadership to avoid fragmentation.

Some ministries have pulpit/congregational sharing of leadership. On the surface it may appear that this structure provides a system of checks and balances, but in reality, such a system breeds hindrances and interferences. The responsibility for a vision and its implementation must rest with the visionary leader. Other leaders and the congregation can only assume an associate responsibility.

Cooperative Ministry

The function of key staff is significant to the overall operation of a ministry. This is especially true in the case of the executive secretary. Since some staff positions are afforded a close relationship with the primal leadership due to the nature of their work, levels of influence are created. Control of the appointment schedule means control of the traffic that flows directly to the leaders. The climate of a ministry can even be thermostatically controlled by the one who answers the telephone.

Few staff members are afforded the ease of entry into the presence of primal leadership at even the most critical times as a secretary. Whether delivering refreshments or a telephone message or taking notes, the secretary is afforded the privilege of confidentiality. The secretary is the watchman and trusted guardian who shields the primal leadership from the unwanted, the unnecessary and the untimely. Secretaries are the implementors, gatherers and storers of information. Letters written or received are at their discretion. The most urgent matter can be demoted to *file thirteen* in a brief moment. What power!

At times secretaries serve as buffers between intruders and pastors. Running interference, they are called upon to give a reason (or at least a good answer) as to why a letter was not answered or a telephone call was not returned. They are the confidants who are privileged to the vulnerable thoughts and actions of the decision-making process.

Often secretaries face manipulators who offer them flowers, cards and candy for an appointment with the leader. Hence, they must constantly be on guard to exercise their task with fierce discretion.

Because they are in positions of influence, they are also presented with tremendous challenges. One such challenge is resisting the tendency to be controlling. Since they monitor the traffic flow of people and information, they inadvertently contribute to the decision-making process. Pastors need to be sensitive in not expecting decisions or duties from their secretaries that are not within the realm of secretarial responsibility.

If the key leader is away from the church, it is important that the associates keep that leader before the people. Associates report to the congregation of the senior pastor's activities and also his desire to be with them. It is equally important that the primal leader give strong consideration to the amount of time that he is away from his church, especially on Sundays. If the congregation feels that a leader desires to be with them more than away from them, they will tolerate occasional absences. Where multiple leadership work with a key leader, it is important that the ministry and even the itinerary of the primal leader be accentuated.

A ministry gifted with the fivefold ascension ministries tends to attract people to the vocal and prophetic ministry. Hence, if the resident prophet is not the senior pastor, care must be exercised in maintaining a balance between the administration of the pastoral and prophetic ministry—especially when the congregation is prone to exercise these kinds of preferences. Zeal, enthusiasm and lack of wisdom in exercising of spiritual ministry to the degree that it usurps a complementary ministry becomes a loss in effectiveness to all. Communication between the ministers is the key.

Leaders are understanding how multiple or plural leadership functions under a definite head. An interesting concept arises when the key leader is viewed as a visionary and the associate staff as implementors. Dreamers see the whole scheme of things. They operate in one time frame, *Now!* If they get bogged down with the nuts and bolts of their ideas, they can become ineffective.

Implementors may not always see the entire picture. They are probably most effective when they have *tunnel vision* that provides a focus in achieving their tasks. Because of this tendency, friction often exists between the visionary and the implementor(s). The implementors cry out, "Don't they know we don't have enough money for that project!" Or "We are still working on the last thing you told us to do!" Of course, the dreamer's cry is simply, "Come on! Let's get this done!" Here again, honest and frank communication is necessary. Also the gap must narrow between the visionary and the implementor.

If the energy of the inspiration far exceeds the energy of the implementation, then stagnation sets in. Responsiveness on the part of implementors and sensitivity on the part of the visionary is necessary. Reluctance to act on God's direction on the part of the staff or people is not a tool of direction for a ministry.

A noted pastor and author remarked that during a tremendous time of revelation from the Lord and great blessings in his teaching and writing ministry, he was experiencing a significant decline in church growth and attendance. This was extremely perplexing. Since the ministry of the Word was producing such personal blessings, he assumed that the congregation would share in this abundance. On the contrary, the farther he advanced along that line of ministry, the less responsive the people became. He thought at first that he should stop preaching along the line he was going. However, the matter was so heavy upon his heart that he could not discharge himself from his current course.

During a time of prayer, the Holy Spirit impressed

upon his mind that the people were lagging behind at the last watering hole. They were content to receive ministry that catered to their needs. Since he was now preaching things that would move them beyond their emotions into a posture of accountability for something beyond themselves, they were unwilling to go. This pastor had to go back to the watering hole and get them, understand their reluctance, and gently bridge that gap between them and himself. During this period of transition, he continued to give them some of the *old water* while he also administered the new. The church quickly assumed a growth pattern once again.

Leaders must be strong in their convictions. However, leaders must recognize a danger in surrounding themselves with associates who will not be honest and open toward them. It has been my experience that strong leaders desire honest and open communication with peers and associates. They only require a right attitude and spirit in the communication process. Associates cannot fear reprisals or rejection for being true to their convictions. Honesty should never breed a spirit of disagreement. But if decisions in a ministry rest with a multitude of counsel, then intimidation of expression will spell genocide for the work.

Once again, open expression calls for a delicate balance between individual views and the necessary respect due a primal leader by his associates. That respect should never be violated even in open communication. Every leader looks for pockets of trust, confidence and reliability among associates. It is comforting to know that betrayal is not simply when people disagree. Betrayal also means the violation of trust or the violation of the confidence to be honest and truthful. If an open atmosphere exists, the primal leader will have the right to vent his own frustrations and concerns without the fear that he is suppressing the opinions of his associates.

Children have a tendency to be very open and frank with one another regarding their opinions and feelings. They feel no threat of reprisals. They are not as open and frank with their parents in the communication process, because they choose to avoid the consequences of such frankness. This process of communication is quite observable in the corporate communication process as well. Often in ministries associates neglect a particularly vital function in the decision-making process—truthfulness.

This missing step in no way is an indictment of dishonesty. How effortless one may go along with the flow of a meeting when, in reality, he feels honest reservations. If voiced in the proper spirit and manner, objections will be viewed as profitable. Many major decisions are fine-tuned and clarified during periods of corporate vulnerability and openness.

When Jesus asked the disciples to relate to him the observations of others regarding his ministry, He finally asked them one vital question in quest of their honesty: "Who do you say that I, the Son of man, am?" At that point He wanted honesty. He was also searching the depth of their comprehension.

In the search for truth and the mind of God, every leader desires honesty from associates called into the ministry alongside him. The challenge to associate leadership is to maintain a proper spirit of respect, honor and truthfulness in fulfilling their ministries. There is a delicate balance between independence and cooperation in maintaining personal integrity. Integrity must be maintained.

Submission simply means following instructions. Submission is not an abdication of the right of choice nor a negating of the decision-making process. Submission is not merely an attitude of agreement. True submission is the highest level of honesty and integrity. The individual negates his personal benefits in an effort to reflect the character of the Lord Jesus in truth.

In true submission personal ambition will no longer be the motivating force. A submitted person is motivated by integrity. Some people confuse submission with a posture of subordination of personal views for the sake of unity. Since true unity is only borne out of truthfulness, genuine submission requires truth, honesty and personal integrity.

Authority is a posture of service. Jesus asked a profound question of His disciples: "Who is the greatest; he that serves or he that is served?" Their obvious answers could have been, "He is the greatest who is most forceful, creative and persuasive." Obviously, Jesus was writing upon the tablets of their hearts. He said, "He that will be great among you must be the servant of all."

I have had the privilege of serving under one of the most effective leaders that this century of the Church has produced. He is a bishop with tremendous responsibility. But above all his accomplishments, he is willing to serve. That is the mark of true authority. To serve is to care, to listen, to give. Authority means giving of yourself and your ministry to others, going the second mile and taking abuse for the sake of the gospel. True service is a state of the heart that comes to those who have experienced a genuine encounter with the Lord Jesus.

Authority is that *worked-in-you* ability to recieve and transmit the life of Jesus Christ, whether it be the life of His character or His words. It takes this kind of ability to receive ideas, insight and revelation. True authority transmits vision to others in a way that produces a cooperative response. Authority does not always mean success in causing those who hear to obey. But authority does mean that out of a willingness to be honest, truthful and unpopular, choices become mandatory. Authority is obedience to God that eventually expresses itself in service to man.

As ministries grow, new demands are placed upon the leadership and staff. Challenges also increase. The quest of pursuing a vision of God will usually leave a trail of disagreement, misunderstanding and hard feelings. Success calls for weathering these storms. Unfortunately, all of the people who are *not of us* do not leave us to prove that they are *not of us*. In fact, many of them choose to stay.

Leadership is challenged to be sensitive to genuine grievances and complaints without being controlled by them. No one can put a *burr under your saddle* like a congregational or staff member. Their unkind words seem to go right past the defenses into the heart. Some remarks express genuine concerns, while others are simply critical, judgmental words and actions that undermine the credibility of the organization.

Here is a place for secretaries or associates to exercise great sensitivity in guarding key leadership from unnecessary encumbrances. At the same time they must make them aware of the *spiritual temperature* of the congregation. When letters or calls come into the office, necessary matters must be differentiated from those which are unnecessary, unwanted and untimely.

However, letters and calls that indicate an unhealthy pattern can be presented before the key leader by a secretary or associate in a profitable manner. Ignoring answering some complaints as a low priority is not a matter of hiding information nor of over-shielding primal leadership from reality. All matters must be put in their proper context. Grievances and complaints ought to be placed in context along with accolades and praises.

When grievances exist among associates or staff, church members will express their observations by decreasing both attendance and financial support of the ministry. The staff demonstrates similar characteristics. Sometimes disgruntled staff avoid regularly scheduled meetings. Perhaps they even schedule secret meetings on their own apart from the normal schedule. Their behavior and performance becomes conspicuous and continually disruptive.

Since the motivation behind such activities is sometimes unknown even to the individual(s) involved, it may be advisable to avoid a confrontation. Instead deal with the broader issue of group dynamics, stressing the integrity of ministry demonstrated through the need for cooperation in attendance and the spirit in which duties are performed. When dealing with such matters of integrity before the entire group, an errant staffer or associate can correct his own ways. However, if this is not the case and a corporate gathering proves ineffective, a more direct approach must be arranged.

Since the development of leadership involves the shaping of attitudes and character, it is advisable for primal leaders not to be provoked too soon or to become reactionary to actions which may at times be resolving inner conflicts.

The need for interaction between primal leadership with the support staff and associates cannot be over-emphasized. Understandably, factors and availability can be a problem. Nevertheless, a planned consistent mode of interaction can facilitate the kind of environment that joins hearts and minds together. Such opportunities should be given strong consideration. Needless to say, as time progresses and strong bonds are established, the nature of such meetings will change.

In the communication process, leaders must master their ability to control situations to bring about appropriate conclusions. Some people react to the negative connotations of leadership being controlling or manipulative. Any effective leader must be somewhat able to maneuver the discussion of a matter to a positive end.

Leaders have the ability and persistence to ask the right questions long enough until the correct response comes forth. They set the correct agenda or theme for a group to facilitate the productive participation of that group. They press for commitments and responses from people when they are operating below their natural and spiritual potentials.

No effective leader desires to be totally controlled by his personal opinions and desires. He will surround himself with associates who will be forthright and honest with their input. In a multitude of sincere and honest counsel, there is indeed safety.

Understandably, at times the decision process must rest upon the shoulders of the primal leader alone without the interaction of others. Moses went up to the mount of God alone without any of the elders. The question posed by many of the unwise was, "Does God speak only to Moses?"

At times a leader will receive input only from the Holy Spirit into his own spirit. To allow for the input of flesh and blood at those times potentially produces a lack of confidence in a leader to hear from God. Those will be critical times in a ministry. It is important that eldership is built on foundations of trust. Certain decisions seem to violate the plurality of eldership or the multitude of counsel. Nevertheless, sometimes that is the Lord's way.

Vulnerability of Ministry

One of the secrets of successful ministry is developing a way to effectively communicate information to people. Information gives people the ability to have *hands-on* involvement in the work of ministry. People must know how they can become involved in fulfilling the vision or theme of a work. Good communication requires that the visionary information be presented in a way that people can relate. Small home cell meetings or similar gatherings providing the opportunity for verbal interchange would probably be a convenient way to allow input from people. Leaders also discover possible channels of expressing their people's potentials.

People desire to be involved if they are shown the way to participate. Too often the use of terminology becomes an issue. A visionary conceives a vision in spiritual language that is as difficult to translate as he perceived it. Hence, the language of the vision must be transformed into graphic, audible and visual modes. Definitions allow God's direction to be perceived by others who did not have the privilege of experiencing the emotions and impact of the original vision.

A visionary can express the emotion and magnitude of his divine encounter, but it is not always possible for listeners to enter into the experience at the same level. Once again, the vision must be made plain, rehearsed and discussed until people recognize their ability to have *hands on* involvement in the process.

A leader needs to identify with people so that they perceive his humanity. In the early phases of ministries there is a great tendency for close relationships to develop since people are few. Leaders make efforts to form bonds of love and friendship. However, close relationships breed familiarity and at times obligations may hamper a growing ministry later when opportunities for such interaction are limited. Those who were given free access to the leader during those early years cannot understand why that access is limited now just "because we are a growing church." Interaction that breeds dependency and harbors obligation should always be avoided.

In a conversation with a pastor and his wife about this issue, the wife made an interesting observation. Because their church was young and growing, frequently they would have a meal with a couple in their church after church services. Occasionally they would visit the couple's home and share in some recreational activities such as tennis or swimming. She paused in the conversation and asked, "Are you saying we should stop fellowshipping with this couple simply because they are not our peer level in the ministry?"

The answer was obviously *no*. The pastor and his wife were encouraged, however, to excercise caution in exposing personal struggles or matters of church business on these social occasions since such disclosures could possibly interfere with their ability to minister effectively to this couple. The choice of participants in the inner circle rests solely with the leader. However, great care should be exercised in selecting those with whom leaders are vulnerable.

The Recognition and Development of Leadership

The recognition and development of leadership is critical to a growing ministry. Leadership selection provides for the continuity of the work after the founding team is gone. It is important to recognize that leadership selection is not a democratic process of equal opportunity that gives everyone a chance. Rather, it is a matter of *putting the best foot forward.*

Ministries with multiple leaders fare much better by exercising this principle of natural selection of the most able, all other things being equal. If one is given to preaching, another to administration, while another to music and another to working with youth and education, then choose the *best foot* and put it forward.

Such a mini-structure greatly relieves stress and strain. Everyone is not given to public proclamation or singing or praying, and the differences become quite obvious when attempts are made to be democratic in the leadership process. Experience has shown that people who volunteer are not always the most qualified. Furthermore, the most gifted people are rarely the ones who volunteer.

The ongoing integrity of a ministry can only be maintained if provisions are made for the continuation of leadership after the founding fathers and mothers are gone. Ministries are conceptualized through the vision and work of an individual. The work will surely perish unless provisions are made for the transfer of leadership to the next generation.

Obviously, no succession of leadership is blessed without the approval of the Lord. The natural sons of Samuel and Eli were somewhat of a disappointment, but their sons cannot serve as a disclaimer to all familial succession in ministry. Many ministries frustrate the grace of God by patronizing jealous non-family peers, and thereby not developing the gifts and callings of God within a son, daughter or relative. Successful ministry will be those who recognize and develop the callings of God wherever they reside and release them to function.

Personal Challenge

Ministry always holds challenges. Paul often made reference to his personal struggles with accusers, false brethren, and even the saints. And then Paul says, ". . . besides the other things, what comes upon me daily: my deep concern for all the churches" (2 Corinthians 11:28). Intimidations, fears, apprehensions, wonderments, rejections, failures and reprisals are the beginning part of a list of experiences that constitute ministry. Leaders can challenge the devil, take on a building program by faith, and preach and prophesy the Word of the Lord to tens of thousands of people without reservations. But personal enemies who seek to degrade character and integrity can be the greatest challenge.

Discouragement enters the scheme of things and causes one to make poor decisions and choices. It is possible to get in such a mental state as to become paranoid, insecure, reclusive and reluctant to express even personal feelings and desires. This is the time when true eldership must be found. The cry both of the human spirit and of the Holy Spirit is for fathers and mothers in the Lord. Many ministries can be salvaged when there is the availability of seasoned eldership and the willingness to avail oneself of the proper counsel.

Children are taught that sticks and stones can break their bones, but words can never hurt them. As they grow older and experience life, they discover that indeed words do hurt them. Critical and judgmental words enter the heart and produce great hurt.

For that reason, the writer of Proverbs admonishes us to, "keep the heart with all diligence, for out of it springs the issues of life" (Proverbs 4:23). One of the greatest dangers in the ministry is the attempt to minister from a wounded spirit. A broken and contrite spirit which has been cleansed of pride, arrogance and selfishness is always profitable. But a heart torn apart by judgmental and critical words feeds the spirit of the minister with unhealthy conclusions. Ministers in trouble must be willing to seek out profitable counsel. Solutions come by praying and then picking up the telephone, or taking a pen and paper and writing a letter. Troubled pastors must take the initiative to get help.

Every ministry needs people who flow in the ministry of encouragement. This is not the gift of flattery nor patronization, but of inspired encouragement. Those who are given insight to encourage by the Spirit know times and seasons, good and evil, and can distinguish between the two. Their ministry is not a flamboyant one, but it calls forth trust and confidence because of its consistency and dedication. Those who have this ministry must arm themselves to be misunderstood by family, friends, peers and foes. Their actions probably will be labeled as self-serving, but they must discharge their ministry with faithfulness.

The little maid broke through the mind-set of Naaman and entreated him to obey the Word of the Lord. The minister of encouragement is versed in the knowledge of people and their ways. He knows how to entreat rather than intimidate, but yet he has the boldness to stand in the face of evil or any resistance. Encouragers are life-givers, a breath of fresh air, pools of water in a desert place. Whoever you are, ". . . take heed to remember the ministry which you have received in the Lord, that you may fulfill it" (Colossians 4:17).

At times you will wrestle with internal fears, insecurities and doubts. Discouragement sets in because ministry is often misunderstood. But remember, your words and actions may be the rudder that turns the entire ship from danger and keeps it on its proper course.

Conformity

Conformity is a very interesting word. Conformity shapes something to a desired form. In watching a news item on the invention of a childhood toy called "Silly Putty," I was impressed with the various modes or forms in which this material could be shaped. The material was very malleable. It could be stretched, squashed, twirled, rolled, etc. The final appearance of this little piece of putty bore no resemblance to its original form.

Every organization has codes of ethics and performance to maintain a sense of uniformity and quality. Conformity in this sense assures productivity, efficiency and control of quality. To some degree the character of the individual is molded. Attempts to correct undesirable traits such as tardiness, slothfulness and insubordination begin with parents, teachers, employers, etc.

The expression of individual liberties is not limited, but individual considerations must contribute to the good of the organization. If the right personality is matched with the right job description, all other things being compatible such as intelligence, abilities and experience, then an excellent product is produced.

Conformity on the other hand can be limiting and destructive if an improper standard of ethics is prescribed. If conformity suppresses natural creativity, initiative and zeal, then it produces a negative balance.

Why Leaders Vacate Their Posts

After being in the ministry for several years, I have made observations that indicate a pattern. My economics professor impressed me with a principle while I was a freshman in college. He said that the repetition of occurences indicates a pattern. That was, and still is, a profound truth. Statistically, observable occurrences in various situations lend themselves to predictable consequences.

What is the reason people leave their assigned posts? Obviously there are logistical reasons for moving on to something better. Still, when a divine mandate indicates the completion of one task and the beginning of another, why do people leave? First, there is a lack of the original fruitfulness and inner drive. When divine innovation turns to famine, we assume our work is completed, the vision is fulfilled. Forgive me if I do not dwell on correct reasons for the problems, but rather, I'll focus on some of the real but faulty ones.

King David was a formidable leader and a man after God's own heart. He was fearless in the face of the enemies of his nation. Before Goliath, he was unrelentless and fearless. In the face of the bear and the lion that sought to attack the little sheep herd over which he was given the responsibility, he lacked no courage. But David, like most of us, didn't handle his personal enemies very well. When the attacks were directed against his own character or threats upon his life, David failed. When the accusations were leveled against him with no basis for truth, David reacted.

Is it possible that without fear or intimidation we can face the evils of this world and defeat the enemies of God and of His Church? We cast out devils, heal the sick, stand in faith during building programs and the pains of a growing work, yet we react totally powerless in the face of personal enemies. I dare say that personal enemies and conflicts are the most formidable. With this in mind allow me to develop some of the reasons why people vacate their assignments.

1. **Inability to move beyond personal hurts to a place of forgiveness and restoration.** Whether words are purposed to be a source of intimidation or hurt, they are part of the liability that invariably comes in dealing with people. Anyone involved in the service of people, especially when this brings one in contact with hurting people to develop them into leaders, will invariably have to handle their unkind remarks and words.

2. **Alienation.** Rejection because of a particular stand taken on certain matters; public or private verbal abuse; accusation against your character, integrity, dedication or allegiance; undermining your accomplishments or progress. These are a few of the difficulties. Whether true or imagined, they are among

some of the reasons spiritual leaders leave the ministry.

Abuse hurts where nothing else can soothe. The issue cannot focus on whether the abuses or misunderstandings occurred. The important issue is whether you *will to* weather the storm. Some abusive situations may benefit your growth and development of potential. You will be a better engineer, physician, teacher, fireman, legislator, oceanographer, minister, cook, nurse, housewife, husband, or generally a better person for the process.

Don't overlook the benefits of going through warfare! If you haven't been at this address previously, you could very well get there tomorrow. Remember, though the problem is real or imagined, the critical issue is simply this: will you make life-changing decisions in this frame of mind or heart? Leaving a ministry is not always the best answer. Find an old seasoned warrior walking with a limp who wears some battle scars. Invite him to lunch. Eat more than just the natural food that is set before you. Be open and honest about your feelings. I am sure that he will be graphic about how he earned his limp and his scars.

3. **Unwillingness to handle challenges, confrontations or criticism.** Most people do not handle confrontation and criticism very well. Consequently, many decisions are made out of an avoidance reaction. Emotional pain is delayed or abated by simply leaving. However, it may be helpful to seek the opinion of a multitude of counselors—from a spouse or colleagues—before making a reactionary move.

4. **Great tendency to become fixed or unyielding.** The ability to make changes is a virtue. Although there are times when adherence to convic-

tion is necessary, there are other times when it is more beneficial to adapt to a new pattern, embrace something new or simply drop some preconceived notion. There is a time and season for every purpose under heaven. There is even a time to change. I have known men who had to change their theological presuppositions that they had treasured for years. The change brought about success.

Today many Christians are re-evaluating their theology, especially in regard to a universal worldview and responsible Christian living. This is not a particularly easy time for the Church since the process of evaluation has brought debate and controversy. Yet the mandate is clear: search the scriptures to see if indeed the things which we have dogmatically adhered to regarding the implications of the Kingdom of God are true.

5. **Lack of true perspective of ministry.** Improper balance between meeting the spiritual and natural needs inevitably results in problems. Lack of a proper diet, too little exercise and recreation and even the lack of a confidant serving as a "sounding board" create problems. Imbalances in life create an improper perspective of ministry. Often those attacks of the devil or spiritual warfare are really the product of faulty judgments and decisions due to fatigue.

Ministry is not just a job we do; ministry is what we are. We are not productive simply because our appointment books stay filled months in advance, or because we are in demand around the clock. Without offering a recipe or solution for balance, allow me to offer a diagnosis based on an old home remedy you might have lying around somewhere. Poor decisions can be avoided if we view ministry as engaging the whole man.

Ministry preparation takes time. The frustrations, anxieties and lack of progress tend to be overwhelming at times. Mountaintop highs to valley lows are a part of the experiences every minister encounters in the growth process. Weaknesses and strengths are revealed. And then some people seem to be dedicated to teaching the lessons we never learned alone. All ministers sometimes fall flat and fail at the assignments they undertake. It wouldn't be so bad if we weren't aware of all those glorious things we were supposed to do somewhere in the future. The Word of God is not simply learned by reading and meditating upon it, but by experiencing its contents.

The effectiveness of some ministries depends upon lessons lived out in experiences. Of course, right before the breakthrough is the greatest storm, disaster or experience. In God's grace, He never leaves us without a witness. Most of the time that witness is an experienced saint of the Lord who has walked down a similar road, and who seems to come along at the right time to offer help.

6. **Lack of definable goals or visions.** Every ministry or organization is founded upon a plan or vision with legs put to it. Tenacity, sweat, tears and fears are some of the ingredients of faith. The dominant vision provides the substance for ongoing insight, revelation and action. The vision makes things work.

Subsidiary visions within an organization serve as companions to the primary theme. This is healthy and productive as long as the focus remains on the central theme or vision. Every new idea that comes along is immediately challenged by the mother theme to test its compatibility. The initial responses to "the new kid on campus" are not always final.

A truly compatible vision tends to support and expand the central theme. It surfaces additional adjunct leadership and provides an impetus for work. A new project can be intimidating since it may provide excitement and attract a lot of attention. However, a companion theme to the central vision will always provide new areas of responsibility. A portion of the congregation who has been dormant will find work to do. A key problem is the inability of some to have definable goals within the framework of the overall vision.

7. **The declining dynamics of family and other close contact groups**. Ministry can be a lonely road. Ministers must maintain openness to others. It is so easy to keep our problems hidden inside ourselves, and not to involve anyone else. But closeness with other people is healthy. Closeness enables us to know, to influence and possibly to alter the boundaries of ourselves. A spouse or children can alert a pastor when he is getting away from himself. Honesty allows for checks and balances in life.

Also, small peer groups where genuine honesty and vulnerability flow can salvage a ministry from faulty decisions. Wise men and women surround themselves with people who will be honest without intimidation. Leaders with strong personalities can be intimidating and almost self-limiting. Seemingly, they do not invoke an air of open communication. However, they must feel betrayed when associates and close peer groups fail to provide honest judgments and input.

A noted man of God once gave me some tremendous insight into maintaining balance in my life and ministry. He said, "Be careful when: (1) you think everyone is picking on you; (2) you are not willing to speak your mind; (3) you escape from people and always need to spend a lot of time alone; (4) your sex life is not normal any more; (5) you have an inclination not to fellowship with people or have a good time any more; (6) you feel pressed most of the time; (7) you cry all the time (there is a difference between being touched by the Spirit of God and crying because you are on the verge of a nervous breakdown); (8) you find your schedule is impossible to keep; (9) you begin thinking that food is sinful; (10) you are not sleeping or eating properly." When these symptoms escalate, a leader must be vulnerable to someone such as a spouse or a colleague whom he considers to be on a *peer level.* Don't hide these frustrations. They can contribute to faulty decisions with tragic consequences.

So You Quit Your Job, Huh?

When I was called into the ministry, I received an unusual insight. My calling was not to a traditional pulpit ministry. As a practicing dentist, a calling into the ministry presented many problems. First of all, my Christian friends advised me to abandon the field of dentistry and live by faith instead of leaning upon the world for a living. Second, the religious environment in which I found myself strongly emphasized a separation between *secular* and *spiritual* labor. Those leaders believed that he who preaches the gospel should live by the gospel.

My religious environment and peers were upset with me. I wrestled with the implication of the call and fell into despair and confusion because of all the voices I was hearing.

Consequently, I abandoned the practice of dentistry several times, only to be reconciled back to it by the grace of the Lord extended to me through dreams, prophecies and the wisdom of elders over me in the Lord. God even spoke to me in dark speeches through my accountant. So now, by the wisdom and understanding of my father in the Lord, Bishop Earl Paulk, I am in full-time ministry and maintain a part-time dental practice. This arrangement causes me much less stress emotionally than in the early years of my ministry.

Possibly the call of God upon many men and women is being ignored or misappropriated today because they interpret the call to ministry as filling a traditional pulpit. The Church is not simply made up of preachers. The Church needs teachers, lawyers, doctors, engineers, and numerous other professionals and laborers. Consequently, it may **not** be necessary to abandon one's life work to consecrate oneself totally to the ministry of a church.

While on a mission overseas, my wife, Sandra, and I met a brilliant young scientist and dentist who obviously had a call of God upon his life. He had been warring with this matter of his calling for some time. His church had mandated that a call to the ministry surely required him to relinquish all other life work. He felt that his work among the young people was given to him of the Lord. This conflict with dentistry had immobilized him from pursuing his call to ministry. As we talked, I explained to him the ministry the Lord had given me. My testimony released him to the knowledge that God had called him to both occupations in an unusual way.

I believe in mission work and in people abandoning all for the work of God when God calls them to do that. But the Kingdom of God and the confrontations against world systems will be fought by men and women laboring in various fields of endeavor. Some will not be called to a traditional pulpit ministry. This does not mean their callings are any less valuable to God's purposes.

Spiritual Powers

The release of powers of darkness creating confusion and failure against ministry increases. Oppressive forces come against the minds of leaders to intimidate, to confuse and to create a sense of failure and hopelessness. Whenever a ministry team is put together by the Lord, forces of darkness work to disrupt integrity. People are channels of spirit activity. Various levels of energy and light impact us all. The most unusual realization is that light and darkness can impact the same vessel at different times; that is, the same individual can respond to forces of good and forces of evil. This activity is not possession, but oppression, or spirit influence.

Because man is a spirit being with soul and body, he is capable of responding to various stimuli. For example, suppose there is such a thing as *soul ties,* or relationship bonds formed between people to produce doors of influence. That is, the support and dependency upon an individual can be strong enough to create an unchallenged allegiance. Therefore, that *soul tie* becomes a channel of control and influence of one person over another.

Now, this bond is not always evil or wicked. It occurs quite readily in a marriage relationship. However, such bonding can become a channel of manipulation. When these types of connections get to be exclusive and create unhealthy dependency to hinder other relationships or even decisions, then it borders on what may be called *spiritual jealousy*. This situation is tremendously dangerous in any ministry. It closes off the potential for new ministries to be developed, creates restlessness and resentment, and fosters discord and dissension among other leaders and the people.

Intimidation is a terrible force. To be accused of wrong motives or actions when you know the charge is not true is most hurtful. It is very intimidating to be accused of having a hidden agenda or selfish motives in your work. A person can never prove to anyone his motives or intentions.

Consequently, accusations about allegiance, dedication, motives and the like can be used as instruments to hinder or deliberately divert a ministry. Accusation either by false brothers or by true brothers must never be allowed to provoke an unwarranted response.

A wounded spirit, who can bear? Ministry that flows out of hurts and wounds and devastations can be both positive and negative. If the experience produces wisdom, compassion and understanding in an individual, that ministry is the greater because of a sordid past. But if the experiences have left bitterness and created a wounded spirit that is not healed, dredges of vindictiveness and bitterness become internal pressure points. Those forces attempt to close off the flow of true Spirit-directed ministry. It is probably advisable in such cases to consult with a spouse or peer or someone in whom you can trust with confidence. Wounds, hurts, vindictiveness and bitterness are doorways for influences other than the Holy Spirit.

Good ethical and moral behavior involves choice, not chance. There are always evil forces at work to create what may be called *spiritual set-ups*. Patterned spiritual attacks are *set up* in such a way as to make the individual more susceptible to suggestions and propositions of the spirit world. Such influences do not attack because an individual is evil or wicked or has iniquity within his heart. Rather, Christian leaders may be put in such a posture by spirit interplay that capitalizes on hurts and wounds and anguish of soul and spirit. Such attacks plunge a leader into destructive activity with menacing consequences. This may be the basis behind some ministry splits and moral and ethical improprieties. When people are maneuvered into these positions, they make decisions by provocation rather than instinct or divine unction.

The key to resist such forces is the proper level of vulnerability, channels of communication and trust that respond with spirit acuity. All leaders need called eldership in their lives. Young leadership in the developing phases of ministry must learn to maintain an openness to the senior leadership. The possible development of unhealthy soul-ties during counseling appointments or other emotional dangers in ministry can easily be aborted by healthy communication with those over you in the Lord.

Prophetic Ministry

A significant challenge within the Church today concerns releasing the calling of the prophet and the administration of spiritual gifts. The scriptures make it plain that God ". . . has appointed these in the church: first, apostles, second, prophets, third, teachers; after that miracles; then gifts of healings, helps, administrations and varieties of tongues . . ." (1 Corinthians 12:28).

Furthermore, these ministry offices and gifts

have been given "for the equipping of the saints for the work of ministry, for the edifying of the body of Christ, till we all come to the unity of the faith and the knowledge of the Son of God, to a perfect man, to the measure of the stature of the fullness of Christ . . ." (Ephesians 4:12-13). It appears evident that the duration of operation of these gifts and callings in the Church is wrapped in the phrase, ". . . until we come."

Prophets were part of the foundation ministry of the Church (Ephesians 2:20; 3:5). The prophet was God's voice to bring repentance to His people and insight into the times of reformation and restoration (Acts 3:21; Amos 3:7). (See *Prophets and Personal Prophecy* by Dr. Bill Hamon, Destiny Image Publishers, 1987.) The prophets prepared the way for the first coming of Christ and, likewise, the prophet will prepare the way for the second coming (Isaiah 40:3; Luke 1:17).

Prophets are called by God and not by man (Jeremiah 1:5; Amos 7:14-16; Galatians 1:1,15). Their ministry may be local, with respect to a specific church or trans-local ministry which impacts the body of Christ. Within a local assembly, a prophet may function as a senior pastor or as part of a presbytery or group of elders in that assembly. As part of the presbytery of a local assembly where another pastor heads the work, the prophet functions in a cooperative manner under the headship of that senior pastor.

The prophet has often been viewed as a strange, off-beat character having a temperament like John the Baptist. He has been expected to issue warnings, proclamations, decrees and judgments with a stern face and a roaring voice. He was expected to declare,

"Thus saith the Lord," whether you liked it or not. And of course, the prophetic stereotype seemed to imply that ministry was authenticated by the boldness and sternness of his delivery.

Prophets are not strange, necessarily, in their manner of life or appearance. There are no specific personality types that typify a prophet. Prophets wear suits, blue jeans and tee shirts. They may dine in a fast food place or a fine restaurant. They are people.

In the Old Testament, at times the prophet was referred to as a shepherd. He could execute his ministry and still exhibit the gentle character of God. That is, a prophet could give a prophetic word with a pastoral flavor. This blending of traits explains the verse, "The spirit of the prophet is subject to the prophet." The attitude and manner of delivery is subject to the prophet himself. Many authentic ministries are hindered by a lack of understanding the prophetic calling. A message is not prophetic because it is presented a certain way. Many times because of the weightiness of the message, intimidation provokes the messenger to a reactionary attitude.

I have discovered that prophets use numerous ways to prophesy the wisdom and counsel of God. Many times, if not all, prophecy can be spoken without a "thus saith the Lord." In prophetic preaching, the word of God is declared just as it is in a group meeting. The important issue is that the message of the Lord is delivered in a manner and at a time to give it the greatest possibility of receptivity. How often the Word of the Lord falls to the ground and dies because no effort was made to ensure its growth. I know that there are times when people's hearts are hardened and their ears are deaf. At those times, let it not be said that the prophet lacks tact and wisdom.

In a local assembly the Spirit of God may speak through a prophet, by the gift of prophecy, through prophetic preaching or prayer, or through the spirit of prophecy. These ways are not inclusive of God's channels of revelation, but they are viable spiritual channels that often present problems in the ministration.

When a prophet comes into a local church to minister, perhaps he should inquire of the pastor as to how prophecy is administered in that local church. A church is like a man's house. A visitor must ascertain how matters of life are carried out in that particular home—what is and is not permissible should be clarified to him.

Scripture makes it very clear that we are to know those who labor among us in the Lord (1 Thessalonians 5:12). Anyone who speaks as an oracle of God in a public service is a laborer and an authority. Therefore, in a local assembly, a speaker should be recognized. At least the fruits of his ministry need to be known by the local leaders of that assembly. To come into a local assembly, unknown, and speak prophetically to that people without the eldership's approval stirs controversy. Any church that has a visiting prophet or prophetic minister in its midst would certainly want the privilege of knowing that he sits in the congregation. Certainly, if there is an opportunity to receive a prophetic utterance, it should be encouraged.

Unfortunately, many church services are greatly hampered because spiritual gifts are not exercised decently and in order. Too often during a pause in the singing of a service, a prophetic utterance will come forth. When prophecy is of the Holy Spirit, there is nothing which edifies more. But when it is not of the Spirit, nothing dampens a service more quickly.

There is a strong move of God to restore the ministry of the prophet and prophetic ministry to the Church today. The potential of revelation and insight of these ministries operating within the proper church structure is unlimited. Power comes in the cooperative functioning of the gifts and callings of God. When ministry edifies, the focus of the Church is directed toward the Lord. Then the spiritual temperature of a meeting is heightened as the congregation is ushered into a state of praise and worship.

Although all Spirit-filled believers can manifest any of the nine gifts of the Spirit, all are not chosen of the Spirit to administer the vocal gifts publicly. Some are given to prophetic praying, singing or speaking, while others are not. The recognition of God's gifts and callings is always confirmed by the fruit of the ministry. The Lord is raising up resource ministries to train God-ordained prophets and prophetic ministers on how to function in a local and trans-local setting.

Many potential conflicts between the prophet and the pastor in ministry are due in part to misunderstanding of scripture. The fivefold ascension gift ministries are listed in Ephesians 4:11. But this listing is not according to order of importance. Each of these ministry offices have a different anointing and function. The apostle and prophet are foundational ministries, whereas the evangelist, pastor and teacher perform more personally focused functions. All offices function cooperatively to equip the Church.

Pastors get intimidated by the prophetic ministry because the Church has mistakenly placed an overemphasis on the prophetic word. Indeed there should be no underestimating the power of the prophetic ministry nor the vocal gifts of the Holy Spirit. However, man shall live not by bread alone but by every word that proceeds out of the mouth of God. That general *word* includes the prophetic word, as well as the word of a counselor or pastor. The mind and purposes of God are made manifest in many different ways and should never become competitive. Because of an overemphasis or underemphasis on one area of knowing God's direction, ministries are split.

The pastor works all week to get the saints to church with moderate success. People announce that a prophet will be in town, which results in a tremendous turnout. People will flock to any place where they know God is speaking or moving.

This situation should only provoke the pastor to open himself up to the prophetic realm and also stir the prophet to a greater depth of understanding of pastoral ministry. Let the prophet do the work of a pastor in understanding and implementing his ministry. Similarly let the pastor do the work of the prophet in proclaiming and discharging his pastoral duties. As Paul exhorted Timothy to do the work of an evangelist, so let the prophet and pastor open themselves to the full counsel of revelation of God in the discharging of their ministries.

The prophet and the pastor need not both be in a local assembly. Generally, when the prophet is not the senior pastor, and the senior pastor has an anointing to move in the prophetic realm, there seems to be a greater understanding of the prophetic ministry.

A young prophet or prophetess, unskilled in the way of the Lord in His house, generates controversy in a local assembly. It is advisable to know how things are conducted in a local assembly. Often in a local meeting, it may be advisable to seek out an elder or senior pastor when one feels to exercise prophetic gifts. Once that is done, the responsibility for covering the assembly and judging the spoken word rests with that elder.

The Lord certainly does not direct the Church by prophecy only. As the Bible says, "Man shall live by every word that proceeds out of the mouth of God" which includes the word of counsel, wisdom and discernment as well as prophecy. When it comes to directive prophecy, the burden of delivery rests with the eldership of the church, especially prophecy regarding the direction of that ministry. Members of the congregation may speak by the gift of prophecy or spirit of prophecy to give edification, exhortation and comfort. Prophetic direction for the ministry will only come from the eldership. Why? Accountability before God for the ministry rests with those elders.

Prophecy must be judged by the elders. When personal prophecy is given to a saint, it should be brought before the elder(s). Since there is safety in a multitude of counselors, it is probably advisable that in home meetings or small gatherings apart from the local assembly, where no eldership is present, personal words be brought before the elders.

When a prophet gives a false prophecy or conducts himself improperly in a meeting, that single offense does not automatically make him to be a false prophet. The spirit of the prophet is subject to the prophet. Is it not possible that an unlearned prophetic minister can conduct himself improperly? Is it also possible that fears of rejection or reprisals, personal convictions and even doctrines can influence prophecy?

The prophets of Baal attempted to persuade Micaiah to give a favorable prophecy that would be in keeping with their consensus (2 Chronicles 18:12-13). Notice how these same prophets prophesied lies because of their admiration for men (Jude 16). Respect or personal feelings for others can greatly influence a prophet who has not been dealt with by the Lord (Deuteronomy 16:19; Acts 10:34; 1 Peter 1:17). The point to be made here is first Micaiah gave a false prophecy (2 Chronicles 18:14). Then he recanted. Shall we call him a false prophet? Obviously not! If we shall know ministers by their fruit, we must remember that fruit sometimes takes a while to mature. Sampling fruit before it matures produces some unfortunate consequences and conclusions.

Ministry which edifies elevates the spiritual temperature of a service. Such ministry focuses the attention of the congregation upon the Lord, thereby opening people's hearts to worship. The Holy Spirit is an unselfish Spirit. He not only speaks of Jesus and things concerning the Kingdom of God, but also directs all attention toward the Lord. A false spirit is like its father—selfish, proud and usurping. A false prophet consistently speaks words which bear unhealthy fruit.

The present day judgment of the ministry of the prophet is somewhat harsh because of immature spirits and familiar spirits. Too many sermons are out of touch and lack anointing. But are those preachers without anointing labeled as *false preachers*? Do evangelists ever minister salvation to a congregation of Christians? Is that evangelist called a *false evangelist*?

Nothing is as disheartening as prophecy spoken out of season or delivered in the wrong spirit in the midst of a tremendously blessed time of praise. Nothing is as devastating as a false prophetic word given to someone who allows that word to become the basis of some significantly erroneous decisions. For these and other reasons, the prophet is regarded today either with disdain or with honor.

In a local ministry the proper structure can eliminate much of the controversy in the manifestation of spiritual gifts. Reliance upon a multitude of counsel and the knowledge that every public utterance is to be judged by the elders brings balance. The Lord desires to give insight and revelation into His will and purposes in these days. The Church and its leaders must work together to ensure the proper balance.

We are in a day when God is calling for a greater working together of pastor and prophet in the Church. Revelation, insight and proper methods of implementation cannot come to the Church without unity of mind, purpose and direction.

Qty.	Title	Price	Amount
	BOOKS		
	Spiritual Megatrends	$ 8.95	
	That the World May Know	$ 7.95	
	I Laugh . . . I Cry . . .	$ 12.95	
	Ultimate Kingdom	$ 7.95	
	The Provoker	$ 9.95	
	Held in the Heavens Until	$ 7.95	
	The Wounded Body of Christ	$ 3.50	
	Sex is God's Idea	$ 5.95	
	Satan Unmasked	$ 7.95	
	Thrust in the Sickle and Reap	$ 5.95	
	To Whom is God Betrothed?	$ 4.95	
	Incense and Insurrection	$ 3.95	
	My All Sufficient One	$ 5.95	
	Divine Runner	$ 3.25	
	20/20 Vision	$ 2.50	
	The Second	$ 3.95	
	Sub-Total		
	GA Residents Add 4% Tax		
	Shipping & Handling		$ 2.50
	TOTAL		

MAILING ADDRESS

Name _____

Address _____

City _____ State _____ Zip _____

Phone (_____) _____

Mail complete form with
payment to:

P.O. Box 7300
Atlanta, GA 30357